Old Turtle
Questions of the Heart

A Story by Douglas Wood   Illustrations by Greg Ruth

Scholastic Press • New York

LIBRARY OF CONGRESS CATALOGING-IN-PUBLICATION DATA
Names: Wood, Douglas, 1951– author. | Ruth, Greg, illustrator.
Title: Old Turtle : questions of the heart / a story by Douglas Wood ; illustrations by Greg Ruth.
Other titles: Questions of the heart
Description: First edition. | New York : Scholastic Press, 2017.
Summary: When the people have deep questions about life, death, and how to find happiness, they journey to find Old Turtle, and she answers their questions with wisdom and love.
Identifiers: LCCN 2016016949 | ISBN 9780439321112 (hc)
Subjects: LCSH: Life — Juvenile fiction. | Conduct of life — Juvenile fiction. | God — Juvenile fiction. | Turtles — Juvenile fiction. | Nature — Effect of human beings on — Juvenile fiction. | CYAC: Life — Fiction. | Conduct of life — Fiction. | God — Fiction. | Turtles — Fiction. | Nature — Effect of human beings on — Fiction.
Classification: LCC PZ7.W84738 Olh 2017 | DDC 813.54 [E] — dc23
LC record available at https://lccn.loc.gov/2016016949

10 9 8 7 6 5 4 3 2 1   17 18 19 20 21

Printed in China   62
First edition, April 2017

The illustrations were drawn with graphite pencils on Strathmore 400 series drawing paper and then combined with layers of scanned watercolor to create the final digital paintings.
The text was set in Adobe Garamond.
Book design by David Saylor and Charles Kreloff

To those who bravely follow their own questions of the heart,

wherever the trail may lead

— D.W.

To my dear friend Alex Gargilis, my wise turtle at just the time

when I needed it most, and always the place I climb to when

I need answers

— G.R.

It had been a long time.

So long that many had forgotten or had begun
      to doubt that such a being as Old Turtle
      had ever really existed.

She was only legend, perhaps, a story told late at night

to make the shadows seem less dark,

the evening fires a bit more bright.

But the people had questions, questions that haunted their

      sleep and troubled their waking hours, questions that

      hung like veils of mist, hiding the morning sun.

Questions, perhaps, for Old Turtle.

But how to find her? Even if the stories were true, who knew what road to follow? What map could show the way?

"The Old Woman will know," someone said. For it was the Old Woman's own grandmother, so the story went, who had once found Old Turtle herself, who had made the journey as a very little girl.

So to the Old Woman the people went.

"Yes, the stories are true," she said. "There is such a being,
old as the stony hills themselves. But there is no map to
follow and no road, only the old, overgrown paths,
and the ancient track of the sun and the moon.

"Follow these, and the whisperings of your own heart,
and you will find your way.
Perhaps I can travel with you.
Perhaps I can help."

And so a trusted few were chosen to travel with the Old Woman, to find Old Turtle, to speak for the people and to ask their most important questions.

They began their journey upon traces of the old, familiar trails. When the old paths ran out, they found new ones or made their own.

The people traveled together, yet each carried alone the weight of his or her question. Until finally, guided by the whisperings of their hearts, they found Old Turtle.

"Sit here with me among the flowers," said Old Turtle,

"in the shelter of the trees. Ask your questions,

and I will try to help."

So it was that a young man, uncertain about the
journey of life before him and worried about its
many choices and challenges, asked, "Why are we
here, Old Turtle? What is our purpose in life?"

"Within your question is its own answer," said Old Turtle,

"for the purpose of life *is* life. We live that there might

be more of life in the world. More *live-li-ness*.

More beauty, more generosity, more variety,

more of the gift of life itself.

"Some seem to do this gracefully, almost without effort and without thinking, while others must think hard about their task, about their place in the living world.

"The flowers of this field fulfill their lives in the abundance
    of their beauty. It is the pleasure of the flowers to
    give more than simple need requires. They adorn
    the earth and perfume the air, and they clearly
    say without the gift of speech that life is good and
    sweet, and though sometimes tangled in thorns,
    it is crowned with loveliness.

"Each and every being, *in* its being, is an expression of life, and no one lives alone. We all live for one another, and in doing so we fulfill ourselves — we find our purpose."

A woman with a spark of laughter in her eyes,
but whose face was lined with care, asked,
"How do we find happiness, Old Turtle?"
Gently, Old Turtle answered.

"Happiness is forever sought," said Old Turtle, "but cannot be found, any more than an apple tree can *find* the apples to place upon its branches. Happiness is the unbidden fruit of our lives. It is the harvest of our growth and the gift of our own giving.

"Happiness is the long-chased butterfly that finally lands upon the shoulder of one who has put aside his net and simply stands quietly in the sun. And when it arrives, it lands so softly it is barely noticed.

"But remember, just as the day knows the night, no one can know real happiness who has not also been touched by sorrow. Each is a part of the other, interwoven threads in the fabric of life."

"Please tell us about family," said a young girl.

There was a hint of shyness in her voice,

but her eyes were clear and bright.

"Family is the doorway into the house of life, little one," said Old Turtle. "When you are very young, your family is all the world and everything in it. The stars shine in your father's eyes; the sun rises in your mother's smile. When your family gathers around a table together, it seems that all the world is there. And in many ways this is true. For our family is the world made small enough to hold.

"Family is the breeze that lifts the kite of your

   childhood into the sky, and it is the string

   that ties you safely to the earth. Without its

   string, no kite can fly.

"Family is a living tree, and it is also the root of your

   own young tree, allowing you to stretch your

   branches toward the sun.

"But no family is perfect," said Old Turtle.

   "Sometimes the string becomes frayed,

   the tree stunted or poorly tended. Then extra

   care and support is needed, to mend the

   string, to nurture young roots and lift broken

   branches toward the sky.

"No one can say all that a family is," said Old Turtle,

   "nor does any family fulfill itself completely.

   There comes a time when you learn that your

   family is not all the world after all — that

   the world is wider than any family's arms

   can reach. But this is as it should be. Then,

   perhaps, a new family is begun, and the world

   is once more made small enough to hold."

"Can you tell us about play, Old Turtle?" asked a little boy.

"When you play, you do the work of heaven," said Old Turtle.

"To play alone is to make life's own heart your companion,"
she said, "to learn for yourself the blue of sky and the
green of grass, the feel of the dew upon your feet —
to know that the world was made for you and is
yours to discover, as much as anyone who ever lived.

"But to play with a friend is to find your joy increased, for
if you learn well in the school of play, you will feel
your own happiness in your friend's smile, hear your
own voice in her laughter, and discover the truth that
happiness shared is happiness doubled.

"There are lessons learned in play that can be learned in

no other way," said Old Turtle, "lessons that last all

your life. But sometimes grown-ups forget, and need

children to remind them."

Old Turtle smiled. "Boys and girls must be patient teachers."

A man who sat uneasily, eyes darting, said, "Speak to us of evil."

Old Turtle paused, breathing slowly, and it seemed that all the world breathed with her. Finally she spoke.

"It has been said that what we call evil is simply *live* turned backward upon itself," she murmured. "For evil is the opposite of life, the stunting and twisting of life to dark and bitter ends.

"Where life reaches for light, evil would deny the light's existence. Where life fulfills itself in variety and diversity, each flower and tree growing as it should, evil would impose its way upon all, seeking to remake others in its own likeness, answering only its own selfish desires.

"Where life is large and broad and deep, ever flowing, ever changing, ever giving, evil from the start is small, concerned only with itself, becoming a foul and stagnant pool.

"Something else is often called evil, and that is simply the loss of balance. Not even the good earth, with all its tides and seasons, is in balance all the time, still and changeless. We experience times of plenty and times of hope, times of loss and hardship.

"Yet even when balance seems lost, there remains a greater, hidden balance. Destruction brings renewal. The wild wind that may someday topple these old trees will also open the forest canopy to the sun, that young ones may grow and seek the light.

"It is our challenge to dwell in harmony with this deep, abiding balance at the heart of life, to live not as refugees from darkness, but as seekers of the light."

Now the Old Woman, stooped by the weight of many years and of loved ones lost, asked, "And what of death, Old Turtle?"

Old Turtle's gentle voice became even softer, and her eyes blinked slowly.

"Death is but the shadow cast by our living," said Old Turtle. "It comes to all of us. Yet because we love, it causes much fear and pain.

"Some fear that in death we may dissolve into nothingness, as if it were from nothing we had come. But it is not in the nature of things that something comes from nothing.

"These trees that brush the clouds did not come from nothing, nor do the clouds themselves, neither the rose nor the stone, the river or the raindrop. All the things that *are* come from something and someplace else that *is*. There is no great nothingness to claim us. Rather, in death we merely return to the source of our life.

"Others worry that in death we may be all alone. But our

lives issue forth from a living root that nourishes

every branch and every blossom, each connected to

the other. All those we have ever loved and lost are

blossoms that have bloomed and fallen, returning

to the root that gave them life. In joining them how

could we ever be alone or lost?

"Death is but the shadow that life casts.

It is always with us, and to fear it

is to fear life itself."

The Old Woman's eyes glistened, and for a long time the

people sat in silence, breathing the perfume of the

flowers, resting in the dancing shadows of the trees.

"Now, my children," said Old Turtle, her voice as gentle

as the breeze among the blossoms, "there is one

more question you have not asked, perhaps the most

important one of all.

"It is a question that is asked by every dawn — a question of

the rising sun and of the light that fills the world. It

is a question whispered by the first morning breeze

and by the bird that sings the first daybreak song. It

is asked by the great world all around you and it is

asked by a small, still voice inside of you. If you listen

closely, you will surely hear it."

The little girl spoke. "I do not hear it, Old Turtle.

I don't hear the question."

But the Old Woman smiled. "It is true, my child,"
she said. "Every dawn brings a question, a
question only the heart can hear: Who are
you, and how will you live this day?"

"But where is the answer, Grandmother?"
the children asked.

"We give our answer each and every day," said the Old Woman, "in all that we do, and in all the choices we make. Our answer is there in the ways that we treat one another, in the courage we must find to face a challenge. It is there in our eyes when we choose to look for beauty, and in our hands when we reach out to help someone. It is in our minds when we strive to understand, and in our hearts when we choose to love. It is there, I think, even in all the other important questions that we ask, and in our journey to find the answers."

Then the Old Woman wrapped the children gently in her arms, and held them, and they laid their heads against Old Turtle's great shell.

And softly, so softly it was more a feeling than a sound, they heard Old Turtle say, "You are the answer, little ones. The person you try to be each day is your answer to the whispered question of the dawn.

"Now, my friends, you have traveled far, and you have a long journey still ahead. It was the questions in your hearts that brought you here, and your hearts will guide you safely home. As you travel, remember this: Although the path of life may be hard and rough and winding, there is no question the heart can ask for which it cannot find an answer."

And as the children hugged Old Turtle one last time, as the people began their long journey home, a breeze sighed in the trees, and the flowers breathed their sweetness into the air.

And Old Turtle smiled.